This Makes Me Sad

RODALE
KiDS

I made a big mistake.
I left the gate open.
My dog, Kit, ran away.

Now I have
an awful feeling
inside of me.

I tell Mom and Dad what happened.
They tell me it will be okay.

But I do not feel like it will be okay.
I feel like I lost my best friend.

We get into the car.
We drive all around town.
But we cannot find Kit.

The sun sinks in the sky.
My heart sinks, too.

Mom and Dad make
a lot of phone calls.
No one has seen Kit.

It is almost dinner time.
But I am not hungry.
I feel like there is a rock
in my tummy.

It is a rainy night.
The raindrops look
like tears on my window.

I start to cry.
Dad tells me it is good
to let out my feelings.
I do feel a little
better afterward.

It is time for bed.
Mom and Dad tuck me in
with a teddy bear.

It is soft and warm,
just like Kit.
But it is not the same.
I miss my best friend.

The next day,
we put up signs
all over town.
I see lots of people
with their dogs.

My insides feel
like ice cream melting
in the hot sun.

Later, we drive
to the animal shelter.

Kit is not there.
Mom gives them a sign.

I look at the animals.
I have an idea!

We can collect supplies
for the cats and dogs!

Mom and Dad love
my idea!
They tell everyone
we know.

Soon our house is full of food and supplies for the cats and dogs!

We bring everything
to the animal shelter.
The staff is thrilled!

The dogs bark.
The cats meow.
Hooray!

Mom asks them about Kit.
No one has seen her yet.
I feel funny inside.
I stop to think.

It feels good
to help the other dogs.
But I feel bad
that Kit is still lost.

I have so many happy memories of Kit.
But they no longer make me feel happy.
I feel like a piece of me is missing.

What am I feeling?
I am feeling SAD.

I close my eyes.
I see Kit in my head.
I can even hear
her barking.

I open my eyes.
I cannot believe it.
Kit is really here!

A woman found Kit playing
in her yard!

She is safe and sound.
It is time to bring Kit home!
Hooray!

I was very sad when Kit was missing.
What makes **YOU** sad?